★i am the sky

by TORRE FORREST

ART OF LIVING FOUNDATION

Art of Living Foundation
P.O. Box 5003
Santa Barbara, CA 93150

Dedicated to His Holiness Sri Sri Ravi Shankar

whose grace permeates our lives,

and whose playful ways inspire the

children to love the divine.

contents

The Poses Continued...

Children's Satsang · · · · · · · ★ 55

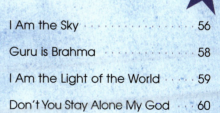

what is yoga?

the children say:

Grace says: It is stretching your body. It feels really good.
        I like to do it anytime! I like to make up my own poses.

Makiah says: I don't know... *You* know what it is! (giggle...)

Tika says: It's something to make your
        bones better and your body too.

Lila says: It's totally fun!

Yoga is so natural–even babies do yoga.
        They stretch like a cobra, they put their
toes in their mouth.
        Yoga is fun!

the adults say:

Yoga has many benefits.

energy level increases with influx of oxygen to the cells.

circulation increases and toxins are eliminated.

immunity is strengthened.

glandular system is normalized.

heart is strengthened and **lung capacity** increases.

digestion and **elimination** are enhanced.

posture improves; **muscles** and **ligaments** are stretched and toned.

mind becomes calm and **power of concentration** increases.

The practice of yoga dates back at least 6,000 years to ancient India. Yogis in deep states of meditation experienced yoga postures arising spontaneously. These were taught to their disciples and passed down through them to us.

breath of joy

I stand up tall and lift my arms, opening them wide - wide - and

leaning back, taking in a deep breath.

Breathing out slowly. I bring my arms slowly around in front,

hugging myself and squeezing the breath out.

Breathing in slowly, I open my arms slowly.

Again, open my chest, head goes back.

Then breathing slowly out, I bring my arms around slowly

and squeeze it out.

I do this a few times - opening, closing. . .opening, closing.

9

rag doll

Standing tall and straight, arms relaxed by my sides.

I let my head and arms droop towards the floor.

My legs are straight.   I hang there for awhile.

Breathing.

I am like a rag doll.

Then I slowly come back up.

tree

I am a tall tree with deep roots.

One leg is my trunk,

the other my branch.

My hands stretch up, up, up...

My fingers are the leaves

and branches at the top.

eagle

Standing tall and strong, I bend my knees,

placing one in front of the other, entwining it around.

I bend my arms, entwining them the same way.

(If I'm standing on the left leg, the right elbow goes under.)

I am an eagle balancing high in a tree.

15

goddess

My feet are spread wide apart.

Knees bent. Elbows bent.

Tongue sticking out, eyes wild.

I am the Goddess.

Full of energy. Watch out!

17

triangle

My feet are spread very wide apart.

My right foot points straight ahead.

My left foot points directly out to the side.

I lean over to my left,

reaching down and touching my ankle.

My other arm goes up over my head pointing to the sky.

I look up at my hand.

My straight arms and legs make triangles.

Then I do the same to the other side.

wide apart

Standing, my legs spread wide apart.

My toes point straight in front of me.

I bend over and place my palms on the floor.

My head goes down, my knees are straight.

down dog

I am like a dog stretching after a long nap.

My feet are behind me, heels pressed down to the floor.

My arms are straight.

My head is down towards the floor.

My back is straight, not rounded like a cat.

cat stretch

Now I'm a kitty stretching my spine.

First I round my back, head down.

Then arching back and looking up to the sky.

I do this slowly,

a few times,

feeling my back

arching and rounding.

camel

I am a graceful, long necked camel

       I kneel with my toes pointing straight behind me.

I curve myself back and hold onto my heels.

            My arms are straight.

I'm pushing my hips forward and stretching my neck back.

lion

I'm crouching on my heels, my arms are relaxed at my sides.

I open my mouth as wide as I can,

making a loud sound a a a a h h h h h h .

Sticking my tongue out.

sleeping warrior

I sit on the floor with both my legs bent back.

I'm sitting between my feet.

Then using my elbows, I ease myself down onto my back

and stretch my arms above my head.

I feel my back stretching and getting longer.

I breathe deeply.

leg stretches

child's pose

I kneel down and then lay on my thighs.

My head rests on the floor,

my arms are behind me.

wheel

Laying on my back with my knees bent,

       I bring my heels in as far as I can, close to my hips.

Placing my palms next to my shoulders, I push myself off the

       floor, straightening my arms, arching my back.

Then I walk my hands even closer

       toward my feet, arching even more.

boat

My legs are stretched out in front of me.

I lean back raising my legs about

as high as my head.

My arms are my oars.

My legs are as stiff as

wooden logs.

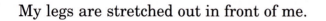

cobra

I am a cobra slinking through the grass.

I lay on my tummy, my palms placed beside my chest.

I raise up off the floor straightening my arms.

My head back, I arch my spine and push out my chest.

I am a cobra ready to strike.

bow

I lay on my stomach

and using my arms, push up, arching back.

My feet come up to meet my head.

plough

I lay on my back and slowly bring my legs up over my head.

My back lifts up,

my feet point behind me touching the floor

and my legs are straight.

I am a plough, making long furrows in the earth.

fish

I lay on my back

and, using my elbows,

push my chest up.

My back is arched.

Then the top of my head touches the floor.

To come out, I lift my head, weight on my elbows,

and then come down.

lotus

Sitting with my back tall and straight

I bend one knee placing my foot onto my thigh.

Gently I ease the other foot over and onto my other thigh.

My palms face up, resting on my knees.

a a a a h h h . . .   I close my eyes and smile.

butterfly

I am a butterfly fluttering among the flowers.

      The soles of my feet are together, close to my body.

  My knees are pressed to the floor.

    I keep my back straight and tall.

      My knees gently flutter up and down.

It's fun to make up your own poses...

grace's pose

I am a tulip.

      I kneel and spread my knees wide apart.

   My feet are pointed together behind me

          my hands pointed in front.

   My head looks up.

makiah's pose

I am an upside-down ladybug.

I walk around on my hands and feet.

shivasana

Laying on my back.

My palms laying beside me, facing up.

I close my eyes.

A A A h h h h h it feels nice . . . sinking, floating.

children's kriya*

I sit with my eyes closed

    I breathe and relax.

Let's see how long I can last...

Three minutes...four...until I begin to....giggle!

I feel so light.

I am the sky.

*Children's Kriya is a breathing practice learned as part of Art
Excel, a spiritual course for children. For information, see page 60.

children's satsang

Satsang means coming together

to celebrate the truth

of our existence—love and joy.

Sing, dance, laugh, play...

guru is brahma

Gu - ru is Brah - ma Gu - ru is Vish - nu

Gu - ru is the great lord Shi - va

Gu - ru is God right be - fore our eyes To

Him my Gu - ru - dev I bow down To

Him my Gu - ru - dev I bow down

i am the sky

Sri Sri Ravi Shankar

I am the sky   I am the o - cean

I   am noth - ing   and ev - 'ry - thing

I'm   the Light   I'm   the love

I   am no - where   and ev - 'ry - where

Ra - ma Ra - ma Ra - ma   Ra - ma Ra - ma Ra - ma

Ra - ma Ra - ma Ra - ma Ra - ma Ra - ma Ra - ma   I

shine in the sun I glow in the moon I'm

glit-ter-ing in the stars, just for you

I'm the breath I'm the life

Come to me, then I'm you.

Ra - ma Ra - ma Ra - ma Ra - ma Ra - ma Ra - ma

Ra - ma Ra - ma Ra - ma Ra - ma Ra - ma Ra - ma

i am the light of the world

Janael McQueen

I am the light of the world and there's on - ly one light

In the blue of the sky

And in the dark of the night In the ba - by's

eyes_____ and in its cries

and I live in the heart of ev - 'ry - one

don't you stay alone my god
Sri Sri Ravi Shankar

Don't you stay a - lone my God Let me

play with you, Let me play with you, Let me

be with you, Let me laugh with you.

Ha ha ha ha ha! Om Gu ru Om Gu - ru

Om Gu - ru Om Gu - ru Om Gu - ru Om Gu - ru Om

Art Excel (All 'Round Training in Excellence) is a spiritual workshop children love, where they learn techniques that help them handle fear, anger and frustration in positive ways. They also learn the art of making friends, the secret of popularity, the value of service to others - all in a supportive, yet challenging and fun atmosphere. It's taught throughout the world by the Art of Living Foundation. To find out more about their programs for children and adults, visit their website, **www.artofliving.org**.

To reach an Art of Living Foundation Center, call or email the national center nearest you: **U.S.A**.: 977-399-1008 (toll free) **India**: 91-80-6645106 Bangalore, vvm@vsnl.com **Germany**: 49-7804-910-923 Oppenau, artofliving.germany@t-online.de **Canada**: 819-532-3328 artofliving.northamerica@sympatico.ca **Africa**: 26-735-2175, aolbot@global.co.za